THE TAILOR OF GLOSTER

MRS TITTLE-MOUSE

SQUIRREL NUTKIN

TOM KITTEN

PETER RABBIT

THE TALE
OF
BENJAMIN BUNNY

THE TALE OF
BENJAMIN BUNNY

BY
BEATRIX POTTER

Author of
" The Tale of Peter Rabbit," etc.

FREDERICK WARNE

*Frederick Warne has a continuing commitment to reproduce
Beatrix Potter's exquisite watercolours to the highest possible standard.
In 1993 and 1994, taking advantage of the latest advances in printing
technology and expertise, entirely new film was made from her original
book illustrations. The drawings are now reproduced with a quality
and a degree of authenticity never before attainable in print.*

FREDERICK WARNE

Published by the Penguin Group
27 Wrights Lane, London W8 5TZ, England
Penguin Books USA Inc., 375 Hudson Street, New York, N.Y. 10014, USA
Penguin Books Australia Ltd, Ringwood, Victoria, Australia
Penguin Books Canada Ltd, 10 Alcorn Avenue, Toronto, Ontario, Canada M4V 3B2
Penguin Books (N.Z.) Ltd, 182-190 Wairau Road, Auckland 10, New Zealand

Penguin Books Ltd, Registered Offices: Harmondsworth, Middlesex, England

First published 1904 by Frederick Warne
This edition with new reproductions of Beatrix Potter's book
illustrations first published 1995

Colour reproduction by
Saxon Photolitho Ltd, Norwich
Printed and bound in Great Britain by
William Clowes Limited, Beccles and London

0799

ONE morning a little rabbit sat on a bank.

He pricked his ears and listened to the trit-trot, trit-trot of a pony.

A gig was coming along the road; it was driven by Mr. McGregor, and beside him sat Mrs. McGregor in her best bonnet.

AS soon as they had passed, little Benjamin Bunny slid down into the road, and set off—with a hop, skip and a jump—to call upon his relations, who lived in the wood at the back of Mr. McGregor's garden.

THAT wood was full of rabbit holes; and in the neatest sandiest hole of all, lived Benjamin's aunt and his cousins — Flopsy, Mopsy, Cotton-tail and Peter.

Old Mrs. Rabbit was a widow; she earned her living by knitting rabbit-wool mittens and muffetees (I once bought a pair at a bazaar). She also sold herbs, and rosemary tea, and rabbit-tobacco (which is what *we* call lavender).

LITTLE Benjamin did not very much want to see his Aunt.

He came round the back of the fir-tree, and nearly tumbled upon the top of his Cousin Peter.

PETER was sitting by him-
self. He looked poorly,
and was dressed in a red cotton
pocket-handkerchief.

"Peter,"—said little Benjamin, in a whisper—"who has
got your clothes?"

PETER replied—"The scare-
crow in Mr. McGregor's
garden," and described how he
had been chased about the
garden, and had dropped his
shoes and coat.

Little Benjamin sat down beside his cousin, and assured him
that Mr. McGregor had gone
out in a gig, and Mrs. McGregor
also; and certainly for the day,
because she was wearing her
best bonnet.

PETER said he hoped that
  it would rain.

At this point, old Mrs.
Rabbit's voice was heard inside the rabbit hole, calling—
"Cotton-tail! Cotton-tail!
fetch some more camomile!"

Peter said he thought he
might feel better if he went
for a walk.

THEY went away hand in hand, and got upon the flat top of the wall at the bottom of the wood. From here they looked down into Mr. McGregor's garden. Peter's coat and shoes were plainly to be seen upon the scarecrow, topped with an old tam-o-shanter of Mr. McGregor's.

LITTLE Benjamin said, "It spoils people's clothes to squeeze under a gate; the proper way to get in, is to climb down a pear tree."

Peter fell down head first; but it was of no consequence, as the bed below was newly raked and quite soft.

IT had been sown with lettuces.

They left a great many odd
little foot-marks all over the
bed, especially little Benjamin,
who was wearing clogs.

LITTLE Benjamin said that the first thing to be done was to get back Peter's clothes, in order that they might be able to use the pocket-hand-kerchief.

They took them off the scare-crow. There had been rain during the night; there was water in the shoes, and the coat was somewhat shrunk.

Benjamin tried on the tam-o-shanter, but it was too big for him.

THEN he suggested that they should fill the pocket-handkerchief with onions, as a little present for his Aunt.

Peter did not seem to be enjoying himself; he kept hearing noises.

BENJAMIN, on the contrary, was perfectly at home, and ate a lettuce leaf. He said that he was in the habit of coming to the garden with his father to get lettuces for their Sunday dinner.

(The name of little Benjamin's papa was old Mr. Benjamin Bunny.)

The lettuces certainly were very fine.

PETER did not eat any-
thing; he said he should
like to go home. Presently he
dropped half the onions.

LITTLE Benjamin said that it was not possible to get back up the pear-tree, with a load of vegetables. He led the way boldly towards the other end of the garden. They went along a little walk on planks, under a sunny red-brick wall.

The mice sat on their door-steps cracking cherry-stones, they winked at Peter Rabbit and little Benjamin Bunny.

PRESENTLY Peter let the pocket-handkerchief go again.

THEY got amongst flower-pots, and frames and tubs; Peter heard noises worse than ever, his eyes were as big as lolly-pops!

He was a step or two in front of his cousin, when he suddenly stopped.

THIS is what those little
rabbits saw round that
corner!

Little Benjamin took one
look, and then, in half a minute
less than no time, he hid himself and Peter and the onions
underneath a large basket. . . .

THE cat got up and stretched herself, and came and sniffed at the basket.

Perhaps she liked the smell of onions!

Anyway, she sat down upon the top of the basket.

SHE sat there for *five hours*.

*   *   *   *   *

I cannot draw you a picture of Peter and Benjamin underneath the basket, because it was quite dark, and because the smell of onions was fearful; it made Peter Rabbit and little Benjamin cry.

The sun got round behind the wood, and it was quite late in the afternoon; but still the cat sat upon the basket.

AT length there was a pitter-patter, pitter-patter, and some bits of mortar fell from the wall above.

The cat looked up and saw old Mr. Benjamin Bunny prancing along the top of the wall of the upper terrace.

He was smoking a pipe of rabbit-tobacco, and had a little switch in his hand.

He was looking for his son.

OLD Mr. Bunny had no opinion whatever of cats. He took a tremendous jump off the top of the wall on to the top of the cat, and cuffed it off the basket, and kicked it into the green-house, scratching off a handful of fur.

The cat was too much surprised to scratch back.

WHEN old Mr. Bunny had driven the cat into the green-house, he locked the door.

Then he came back to the basket and took out his son Benjamin by the ears, and whipped him with the little switch.

Then he took out his nephew Peter.

THEN he took out the hand-kerchief of onions, and marched out of the garden.

WHEN Mr. McGregor returned about half an hour later, he observed several things which perplexed him.

It looked as though some person had been walking all over the garden in a pair of clogs — only the foot-marks were too ridiculously little!

Also he could not understand how the cat could have managed to shut herself up *inside* the green-house, locking the door upon the *outside*.

WHEN Peter got home, his mother forgave him, because she was so glad to see that he had found his shoes and coat. Cotton-tail and Peter folded up the pocket-handkerchief, and old Mrs. Rabbit strung up the onions and hung them from the kitchen ceiling, with the bunches of herbs and the rabbit-tobacco.

THE END